WHO ARE YOUR PEOPLE?

WHO ARE YOUR PEOPLE?

Written by **Bakari Sellers**

Illustrated by **Reggie Brown**

Quill Tree Books
An Imprint of HarperCollinsPublishers

List of historical figures who appear in the book:
pp. 8-9: (from left to right) Muhammad Ali, Maya Angelou, Stacey
Abrams, Martin Luther King, Jr.; p. 11: Harriet Tubman; p. 17: Barack
Obama; p. 18: (clockwise from top left) Serena Williams, Jackie
Robinson, Kamala Harris, John Lewis; p. 19: a buffalo soldier.

Quill Tree Books is an imprint of HarperCollins Publishers.

Who Are Your People?
Text copyright © 2021 by Bakari Sellers
Illustrations copyright © 2021 by Reggie Brown
All rights reserved. Printed in the United States of America.
No part of this book may be used or reproduced in any manner whatsoever without
written permission except in the case of brief quotations embodied in critical
articles and reviews. For information address HarperCollins Children's Books,
a division of HarperCollins Publishers, 195 Broadway, New York, NY 10007.
www.harpercollinschildrens.com

Library of Congress Control Number: 2021946107
ISBN 978-0-06-308285-4

The artist used a little Malcolm (X), a bit of Martin (King),
and a lot of Marvin (Gaye) to create the illustrations for this book.
21 22 23 24 25 PC 10 9 8 7 6 5 4 3 2 1
❖
First Edition

Sadie and Stokely, daddy loves you.
Kai, your (bonus) dad is so proud of you.
—B. S.

To Brittani—she made this world a better
place and will always be missed.
—R. B.

When you meet someone for the first time, they might ask,

"Who are your people?"
and
"Where are you from?"

Who are your people?

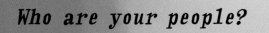

You should always be proud of who you are.

Your people were strong and smart.
They dreamed of things not yet seen and
imagined that we could all be free.

Your people were fighters.

When they were told they had to leave because of the color of their skin, they sat down.

NAACP

WE DEMAND EQUAL RIGHTS NOW!

I AM

NO JUSTICE NO PEACE

We A
ALL
ONE

Your people were mighty activists, champions that struggled for justice and equality.

They marched so that people would know your life matters.

And they stood up and ran to make history and change lives.

Your people were
trailblazers who changed
laws and broke records.

Today we stand on
their shoulders.

When they ask you, "Where are you from?"

You are from a land where the soil is dark and
matches the richness of your skin. Where cotton
and sugarcane were strongly rooted and match your
strength and determination.

You are from the country,
where time moves with ease and
where kindness is cherished.

We say a simple hello to
our neighbors to let them
know we see them.

You are from a place where the aromas of
cakes and pies waft from the windowsills,
to fill your bellies with goodness and your
hearts with love.

You are a product of the proverb "it takes a village to raise a child."

You are from a place filled with love and
hope and expectation. Where people rooted
for you to succeed.

Today we stand on their shoulders.

On their shoulders, you are
so strong and so loved.
On their shoulders, you can
reach for the sky.

So what will you
dream, and how will
you change the world?